MW01484722

THE DEATH OF AZEROTH FIKOR

NURO WOOTERS

Bustard Books - Publisher

Text and illustrations by Nuro Wooters

ISBN: 978-1-7371316-3-2

THE DEATH
OF
AZEROTH FIKOR

BY: NURO WOOTERS

Note to the Reader:

The world in which The Death of Azeroth Fikor takes place is a large land mass in the underworld ruled by six gods each with their own abilities and roles that fulfill and play parts in the lives of mortals, underworldians, and angelic beings alike. The next page is a map of the land in which the story takes place.

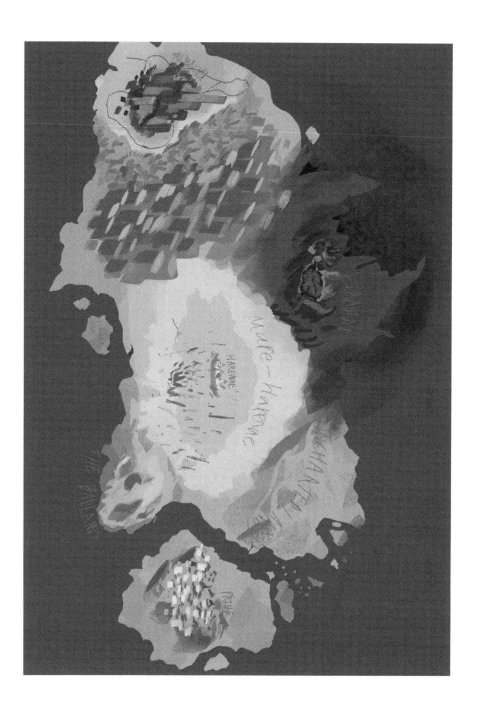

Chapter 1: Winding Paths

A familiar chime rings as I enter Smokey's. It's been five years. Five years since the incident, five years searching for leads, five years. My thoughts are interrupted however by the screech of a stool and a playful voice speaking to me.

"Hey there bud! What brings you into this tavern? Going for a drink? Some grub?" it guessed. I turned over to peer at this strange person, their face washed with a smug expression like a person with a bad poker face when they get good cards, their hands propping up their head like it was about to fall off in excitement.

"The names Aeither, what might yours be feathery fellow?" he questioned.

At first, I gave no response to this figure, I assumed he was trying to sell me something with how he spoke.. And yet words flowed out of my mouth in a hushed mumble.

"My name is Rune." I said. The bartender slid me my ale and I took a sip, however Aeither continued to speak. His tone was no longer playful, yet it was more of a hushed whisper as if he were telling a secret.

"Well, I've gotten word about you and your search.. Do you wish to speak about it with a drink or would a better time suit you?" he inquired. My attention now peaked now that he mentioned my search. *"Tell me, what do you wish to* bring *to my ears?"* I questioned.

His voice echoes again, that same shrouded tone as he spoke of the details. *"I may have a lead, a few connections that witnessed what happened. They live in the city of Prius. Do you wish to come?"* He queried. I thought of my opinions. Another clue. A possible lead? But how can I trust this… strange fellow underworldian..? A sigh escapes my lips. And my hand reaches out to shake his hand in agreement and with a firm grasp the deal is set. I take a final swig of my ale and rise from my seat. He follows as well, with the same energy as a golden retriever as he matches my steps. We step outside and he stands there, staring at me with curiosity and awe. I look back with confusion. He chips in. *"Well, are you gonna do it?"* He asks. I become even more confused. My face twists to slight annoyance. *"Do what..?"* I replied. He starts to do some.. weird arm gesture.. he speaks again. *"Y'Know! Fly so we can get there quickly?"* he says excitedly. I look at him and with just utter disappointment as I open my left wing. Flashing the trimmed charcoal feathers. *"I can't."* I stare at him blankly. His face dropped that excitement that he once had. *"Oh.. well.. that makes this a bit harder then.."* He then seems to think to himself for a moment, rubbing his chin as he paces back and forth before he stops and claps his hands. *"A road trip it is then!"* he states as he gestures to me to follow him. We walked for what felt like hours, through streets illuminated by the streetlights or bright neon store signs, through alleyways, where peering eyes of smokers and store janitors throwing trash away after the day's end, glanced our way, and through streets of bustling shoppers and other pedestrians. There was little to no chatter between us, only the sounds of the cityscape around us filled our ears as we made our way down the subway station near the center of the city. We sat on a bench along the wall, away from the somewhat sparse pedestrians walking in or out of the station. As the empty silence set in he turned to me, a curious glare flickered my way. *"Do the trains usually take this long? I thought with this fancy city they'd have faster travel.."* he queried. I couldn't help but chuckle, he's like a babbling tourist it seems. The one who'd go up to some dangerous group of locals and ask for directions ludicrously. *"The city doesn't care that much for public transport. People just walk or fly to wherever they need to."* I replied. It's quite unfortunate really. For some of the rare tourists who aren't used to walking everywhere, to the fellow flocks whose feathers have also been clipped, or some putridum. I sigh at the thought, but I'm suddenly pulled to reality as the sound of a familiar train horn echoes through the hall. We get up and we swiftly enter the train, there's barely anyone inside besides a mother holding a child in a slumber, an unbothered heron flipping through pages of a novel, and some quiet hooded starling just looking out the glass as the train starts to move. Passing lights in the tunnels shimmer through the windows of the trains as we travel to the edge of Solmacula. After what felt like another hour of sitting around, the fields of the outer city grazed our eyes. The tall grasses are painted with light tans and gold which blur into a blob of yellow as the train swiftly passes through them. Eventually we reached a stop at the farthest reach of the city's territory, the lush golden grasses greeted us as we exited the train into this empty station in the middle of nowhere. We looked around before my eyes caught a path that walked through the grasses, a trail it seemed. I looked over to Aeither and gestured to him to come over. *"Hey there's a trail over here."* I shouted as he scurried over. He nods. *"I think we should go through there; I know a few other travelers this way. Some people prefer to go through the mountains instead of going around them."* he suggests as he makes his way down the worn steps of the station and towards the grass. I followed his steps, albeit with more caution than his confident steps.. A breeze blows through the grasses, giving them the illusion of waves like the sandy sea I imagine is around Herenae. I've never gathered the courage to explore other cities; I hired investigators to travel to them instead, for any info or leads. But I have heard stories of the other underworldian cities, Herenae's lush golden sandy sea, Iraviri's hot springs from the hot lava that flows under it, and Prius's high class buildings and parties. Sometimes I envied the wonders of the other cities compared to Solmacula's. But I forget that it is my home. I've experienced all the glory and dread that it can give me, so I guess my perception of it is blurred. We walked through the waves of grass for thirty minutes before he turned to me as we walked. A curious expression glaring on his face as he speaks up. *"Have you* been outside Solmacula before? You kind of look a little lost." he says before chuckling a bit. Does he find my unfamiliarity humorous? Great.. "Yes.. is it that obvious?" I replied sarcastically in a slight attempt to keep myself from getting too annoyed. He chuckled a bit more. "A bit, yes. But that don't mean you gotta be all cautious with your steps y'know? You gotta taste a bit of risk from time to time." he suggested. That bugs me.. Suggesting that I take a risk after I've taken so many that god knows how many more there are left? I'm not gonna do that. "I'd rather not. I'm keeping my steps careful." I state. He's too carefree for my comfort. I should've just gotten a name and address instead of being dragged along with him. But I was the one that shook his hand after all.. I look back up at him, a softer expression on his face, before he looks back towards the splitting grass. Perhaps he's thinking about his words. Well, time will tell. We walk for another four miles through the tall grass before it starts to become dull. The once golden tall grasses wither to a gray lawn down to our ankles. As I look up, my eyes wander to figures in the distance. Large trees and stone obelisks erupt from the ground, like fingers reaching towards the sky in search of the light. It feels..Eldritch of sorts. Like remains of a past that's impossible to decipher. I look towards Aeither, curious as to if he's experiencing the same kind of anemia as I am. He seems more in awe of the scenery. He takes a deep breath of the oxygen rich air, like the explorers I saw on various nature channels at bar televisions. He turns to me with an ecstatic smile. *"Have you seen anything like this?"*

I step over the shortening grasses to catch up to him. *"I've heard of this place before, from travelers in the city. I didn't know these spires were this massive though..,"* I answered. He chuckles a bit as he turns to look back at the spires, his eyes wander up towards the toppling height of them before they go past the tree line above. *"They'd make a great treehouse or platform house."* He jokingly stated. I couldn't help but chuckle a bit. What a silly thought.. We continue walking, eventually the grasses dwindle down to a thick forest floor, covered in leaves, stones and fallen branches. It was quiet, only the sounds of wind swaying the branches above, and the crunch of the floor below us, echoed out through the surroundings. We approach one of the tall stone spires. Aeither crouches down near one of the larger spikes protruding out from the base of the spire, taking curiosity in one of the small rocks on the ground. I walk over to him, crouching alongside him as I glance at him a bit confused. Why the hell is he so intrigued by this rock? But then he moves his hands toward it, and he lifts it up. Small legs pop out from beneath it and a face lifts from the rock as it chitters and its legs scuttle in Aeither's hands. I grimace at the sight. He looks ecstatic however.

"Hey, it's a little guy!" he exclaims excitedly, a goofy grin plastered on his face as he looks at the small rock critter. *"I think I'll name it Jeremiah."* he stated, looking up at me with the same smile on him. *"We are not taking that **thing** with us."* I scoffed. He gave a playful pout as he set it down. *"Hey, I wasn't planning on it.. Just wanted to make a little note of the guy."* he mumbled as he stood back up, watching as the little critter scurried up the spire, before lowering itself back down, to blend into the stone. I sigh as I stand back up alongside him. We gotta keep going instead of getting distracted by these critters.. or whatever they are. I gesture to him to follow me as we walk around the spire. We continue our path through this forest. Passing the spires that reach for the sky above. I'm tempted to climb up one, just to see where the hell we even are, but from the looks of it, it'd be almost impossible. With my luck I'd end up going up about seven feet and then slip and

break something.. But my mind is drawn back to the path

in front of me, it feels like endless seconds, minutes and

possibly hours pass by us just as fast as the winds that echo

above. Eventually we come to a clearing. A small area lit

by some of the remaining light of the sky, free of the leafy

forest floor and instead lined with about fifty feet of grass.

It's a nice sight, a stark contrast from the forest, that feels

like a refresher for my eyes. We walk into it and I look up.

It's getting late. We must find somewhere to go or to settle

soon or it's gonna be a nightmare trying to navigate this

place in the complete dark. But I'm then drawn to Aeither,

who's looking weirdly at something across the grass. I look

at where his gaze is pointed, and I spot something walking

just behind the trees. A person? No, a creature? It's hard to

tell. Its body is a combination of a man and some sort of

equine. I've heard of them from human literature that's

been collected into the city's library. I call out to the

strange figure in the distance. *"Hello? Who are you?"* I shout. The figure looks towards us, freezing in its steps as it tilts its head curiously. It raises a hand, and waves back at us before turning back to do its own thing, leaning down and picking up some of the leaves and stones from the forest floor. I look over to Aeither, who has an equally confused look on his face as me. We look at each other before he shrugs and continues walking forward. I stay in place however. I glance towards the figure as it leans back up and begins cantering away, deeper into the forest until it's out of my sight. I catch up to Aeither and speak up quietly. *"Do you know what that was?"* I question. He stops to think for a moment. *"I think it was a centaur. I've heard about them, but I've never seen one that close. They are pretty chill though."* he replies as he goes back to walking. Strange, I've never seen one; I always assumed they were something mythical from rural town rumors and legends. One such legend says they used to be ruled over by an old despair god from eons ago, another one says they are cursed Pertrudium who take the skin from living beings after their own greed and gluttony consumes them and their thoughts. But those old town rumors don't seem to be the case to me anymore. We continue, stepping over rocks, passing more and more spires; I've practically lost count of how many we've passed. As I look forward I can see a large accumulation of rocks, odd geometric columns that go up past the tree line like massive steps. As we get closer I look up towards the towering height of stone and basalt. Great, a mountain! We make our way up some of the easiest slopes that we can climb. I dare not look down as we go further up. The light around us dims as the minutes pass, and it gets later into the night. Dusk sets in as the climb gets more and more difficult the higher we go. The stones blend into darkness as the light disappears over the horizon. I call out to Aeither, who's managed to climb higher than me. *"God, I can't see a damn thing."* I complain. He shouts out from above as I heard him take a couple more steps up. *"I think there's a big column up here that we could rest on for the night. Just a couple more steps!"* he exclaims. I desperately try to muster the courage and strength to keep going up this damn death trap of a mountain. He seems to have made it up there before me as I heard him take a couple steps around. I make my way up to the cliff. I grab the sides of the edge as I lift myself up. But as I push up against the edge of the column I feel my leg slip off the edge. I slide down and nearly fall. My heart pounds against my chest as I hold on for dear life. Everything around me falls slowly as my grip starts to slip. But, before I can fully comprehend my damn impending doom Aeither grabs my arm and pulls me up from the cliff and my trance of pure adrenaline and fear. I scramble to sit on the column. He sits alongside me. Everything is silent as he and I just comprehend the event that just happened. My heart still beats fast. It's a strange feeling. One I don't ever want to feel again. It was like the hand of death itself was reaching for my neck. It sends a shiver down my back just from the thought of it.. Aeither turns a bit to look at me. *"You.. uh.. Are you alright there?"* he murmured, a soft smile on his face as he voiced his concern. I think he's just trying to lighten the dreadful mood. I nod. *"I.. I believe so,"* I muttered out. I look down at my hands, which are trembling in place. He seems to notice that, as he reaches behind and unclips a small canteen from his belt and uncaps it. He holds it out to me. *"Here, take a drink bud."* he mutters. I shakily accept the canteen and take a few sips. The lukewarm water is soothing. I hand it back to him with a thankful nod. *"Thanks.."* I mumble. All falls quiet once more. The winds from the distant coast continue to blow past us as we sit there. "*We.. should probably get some rest..,*" he murmurs as he moves to lay down on the floor. I nod as I turn to lay on my side. My eyes close slowly as I rest for the night..

Chapter 2: Endless Sands

I'm jolted awake by the sound of Aeither uncapping his canteen. I groan as I lean back up, I stretch my arms and spread my wings, and yawn. Feels like I barely got any rest.. My back is killing me from sleeping on this.. damn rock. Aeither chuckles a bit. *"Not a morning person I assume?"* he queries. I groan in annoyance. *"Yes, I'm not a morning person after nearly dying yesterday.."* I hissed. He sighs, seeming slightly brought down. He stands up and stretches a bit. *"Well, you have a point there.. But you're still living. So may as well keep living it."* he states as he reaches out his hand to me, offering to help me up. I sigh as I take his hand; he did technically save my life after all.. As he helps me up I give him a thankful nod. Hopefully I can find a way to pay him back for that later. We start on our way back up the mountain. I go first as I reach for the closest stones and places to step. In the distance I see some more critters. Their heads look similar to picked tools.

They chisel into the stone before using their beaks to dig into the hole for any insects or creatures beneath the surface. They look like they'd be a blacksmith or a miner's best friend. I chuckle at the thought. We continue upwards, sometimes making pit stops on some of the larger columns, before continuing to catch our breath. After about an hour or so I managed to scramble up a massive pillar. As I look out into the distance, I'm greeted with the slow dwindling of the columns below before they mix into the environment of dust and sand. The Mare Harenae.. Or what's before it. The golden grasses we saw earlier were like a sign of what was behind the mountains. It was.. Oddly serene. I look back at Aeither who is now just catching up and I gesture for him to come over. As we both look out, the winds pelt us from behind. I look to my left, and there I can see in the distance, the massive mountains and spires that surround the city of Iraviri. It feels.. strange to know that the cities are this far apart. It's like Solmacula is secluded from the rest of them because of this mountain.

I wish Azeroth were here to see this. I think she would've loved it. She was always one for nature. She decorated the house with vines, plants, flowers, anything natural that suited her taste. My mind is dragged back to the present however, by Aeither, who's starting to climb back down the mountain. I follow him, making careful steps down the mountain's columns. It took a lot less time getting down than it did going up. It was a more casual slope downwards than the steep hill on the other side, and I was quite thankful for that. We eventually make it to the bottom. We walk toward the beginning of the desert, going through the small patch of tall grasses before it dwindles down to sand. I savor the warm particles beneath my talons with each step. I look up, and in the distance I see nothing but a golden sea of sand in front of us. We walk for what feels like hours, the further we go into the desert, the more I start to dread the warm sand. It gets hotter and hotter the further out we walk. It doesn't help that my damn feathers are darker than most. So, I end up absorbing more sunlight like a dark sidewalk in the city. My wings are practically a searing hot grill. Even if I raise them above my head to keep my body decently shaded it doesn't help the searing heat around us. I look over to Aeither, who looks like he's getting badly sunburnt and is sweating buckets. I guess that excitement he had at the top of the mountain had dwindled down significantly.. We drag on for miles. The sand which was once just a comfortable warm is now searing hot as the sun beams down on it. As I stop for a moment to catch my breath I turn over to Aeither. He looks really tired.. And it seems I was correct because as I look at his face I watch as he just falls over. I stumble over and drag him along. But even my exhaustion and dehydration take over me. As I also fall to the ground, I roll over. The hot sand now against my wings as I look up at the beaming sun. Are we gonna die out here? That's all that's running through my mind as I barely can keep my eyes open. As they close. I hear the wind passing us and then,.. Nothing.

Chapter 3: The City of Sand

I slowly awake. Groaning as I sit up and recollect what even happened.. I remember I was in the desert, but where am I now? I rub my eyes and open them. It seems I'm in some kind of med bay or something.. I look to my left and Aeither is in the other bed just snoring away. At least he's safe I guess.. My thoughts are drawn to a halt as I hear the door creek open. I look over to see a tan Rextile enter the room with a tray in its hands. On the tray is a pitcher of water and two ceramic cups. As they look over at me they seem to be surprised. *"Oh, you're up!"* it blurted out as it walked over to the small counter in between the two beds and set down the tray. It pours some water into one of the cups and then pulls a small stool over to the bed and sits down in it as it holds out the cup to me. *"Feelin' alright? I found you guys passed out in the sand like dryin' fish on a shore after jumpin' out of the water."* it politely questioned. I accept the water and take a sip before I look back up at them. *"Yes, but I gotta ask where we are?"* I replied before taking another sip of water. *"Well, uh.. This is the west medical center in Herenae. Were you trying to get here for somethin' or....?"* it asked. Herenae? At least we were closer to Prius... I sigh a bit as I set down the water on the tray. *"We're actually trying to get to Prius.."* I muttered. I feel a bit embarrassed for having to end up being dragged to Herenae by this stranger because we passed out.. But I do appreciate being saved. I think if he didn't see us we'd be dead. *"But I must say thanks for saving us out there."* I mumbled. He nods *"ah no problemo. Also, uh, I must get your names for the medical documents. The nurse at the front desk was not very pleased with me when I said I didn't have your guy's names for the records."* he added, scratching the back of his head a bit as he spoke. I nod. *"I'm Rune"* I replied, before I turn to point at Aeither, who is still snoring away loudly. *"And that's Aeither."* I added. He then nods as he reaches out for a handshake. *"The names Maple, pleasure to meet ya'."* he announced. A smile on his muzzle as we shook hands.

"If it's not too forward I wanted to ask.. What kinda' business y'all got at Prius? Goin' for the parties or visitin' a friend or somethin'?" he questioned. I debate in my head about telling him why, exactly, we were going. Maybe he knows some directions or a way to get there that doesn't include us drying up in the sun.. *"Well, we're looking for someone.."* I muttered. Maple curiously cocks his head to the side; he seems to think for a moment before he nods. *"Ah alright! Hey, I gotta deliver some stuff in that area, I could take ya'll there with me."* he suggested. I nod, we're gonna need any help we can get to cross the Mare Harenae.. I then look over to Aeither who seems to be stirring awake. I sigh as I get up from the bed and stretch a bit. I look over and it seems Maple's turned his attention to refresh Aeither with some water from the pitcher. It takes a couple of minutes for us to get ready to leave the medical center, as we first had to make sure the documentation was

all written down for our stay. Maple leads us to the front desk where we have our names and basic information, such as species, our patron, and such written down .. By the time we are done, it is late afternoon. As we step out of the medical center it takes a bit for my eyes to adjust to the brightness of the sun. but as I do, my eyes are greeted by the bustling city of Harenae. Lightly colored tiles mark the paths and the streets, which are lined with dozens of shops and small markets. Glassblowers, smiths, tailors, nearly every service can be found here. It felt.. homey of sorts. It was crowded, yes, but it provided my eyes a plethora of sights to see: other rextiles, fellow followers of Valarie, including a band of rextiles playing music to a bustling crowd of dancers, twirling in pairs with silk sheets connecting them in their dance like flowing ribbons. It was mesmerizing to watch; the vivid colors of the long dresses and flowing robes were like a river of life that can only be found here. It reminded me of Azeroth, the sight emitted the same bubbly energy that rubbed off on me whenever we danced together, the feeling that I was rubbing the fuzz of a peach or a soft blanket over my fingers. It's strange to feel it again after all this time. I'm tempted to go over and ask if I can join this crowd of dancing people, but I don't know the steps of their dance. I snap out of my mesmerized trance once I realize I'm nearly losing Aeither in the crowds of people, and I hurriedly rush through them to catch up. As we walk further into the city we seem to reach the center. A large fountain is placed in the middle of the circle in this area. A bright light is illuminated through a small crystal orb at the top of the fountain, sending a beam of light into the sky like a powerful beacon. I wonder where the light is coming from. Possibly something underneath the city? I'm not entirely sure myself but I can't help but feel curious about it. Maple seems to notice my curious look and steps next to me. He points a finger at the orb at the tip of the fountain.

"Y'know, there's a rumor around here that these lights are from Azulons Keep?" he explained. *"Azulons Keep? He's the God of Guilt, am I correct?"* I added. I feel as if I've heard of his name before, maybe in some of the historical scripture in Solmacula. Maple chuckles a bit as he leans to whisper to me. *"Yep! I've heard he's always busy with managing the overworld beings, working twenty four seven just to keep his work at bay.. He's a workaholic if you ask me.."* he muttered. It seems pretty amusing that such a being with that much power is actually just a workaholic.. Are all the gods and deities like this..? It really makes me think about Valerie. I've never seen him in person, only in papers published by his-to-be successor about his health, plans for the city along with Bezzle, and other small snippets of his life. The God of Lust seems a lot more

professional than his job suggests. But for now, I settle my thoughts as we keep walking through the city, passing restaurants, shops, hotels, and houses filled with liveliness that I haven't seen in forever. Eventually Maple gestures us towards a stable. As we enter, he walks over to one of the stalls and appears to be guiding something out of it with a lead. A large Camsal steps out alongside him. Its light tan scaled skin glistens as the light from one of the windows hits it. It lets out a bellow as Maple pats the snout of it. The large blade-like horn on its forehead is quite intimidating; it's a wonder it hasn't torn up the wooden supports in its stall.. Maple then moves to pick up a saddle that rests on the side of the stall door, and he straps it onto the Camsal's back and gestures to us to help pack up the delivery. Once everything was set, Maple climbed up on the saddle and helped us mount as well. And with that we made our way out of the stables, out of the city's walls and into the sandy wasteland outside. I look out to the golden sands in the distance again with less enthusiasm than I did before. It feels twice as hot as when we first came here.. And before we know it, Maple's Camsal dives down into the sand, swimming through the ground below us and slicing any larger rocks with its horn as it moves swiftly. I hold on for dear life as this thing glides through the sand. Aeither looks utterly ecstatic by the speed and the wind pelting his face. If I even open my wings a bit I'd end up flying off from the sheer speed we're going across the mounds of sand. Every now and then I check back on the crates we loaded on the back of the Camsal, making sure that we haven't lost anything with the damn speed we're going. As I look forward past Maple I see tall blue glass spires in the sand, like massive nails that protrude up from the ground. Their structure is…strange. It looks like whatever created them happened rapidly, bringing the sand upward, melting it and then instantly hardening into a shiny, transparent, blue spire of glass.. Maple senses my curiosity and looks back at us. *"See them spires? We call em' fulgar spires. They happen whenever a lightnin' storm passes through here and strikes the sand."* he shouts. The wind makes it nearly impossible to hear, but I get the basic gist of what he's trying to explain. They look really neat; however, my attention is drawn to the collection of clouds further ahead of us. They swirl in a spiral as they begin to darken. *"Speakin' of lightin' storms, seems like we got one ahead. I'd hold on tight if I were ya'll."* he shouts. My grip on the saddle tightens but Aeither turns to me. *"Hey, pass me those binoculars on the holster back there."* he says, holding out a hand for the binoculars, which I hesitantly lean back and grab. I set them in his hand, and he turns to look at the storm ahead. His expression seems to light up as he sets them down. *"Definitely some lighting up there!"*

he announces. Maple nods as he holds the reins a bit tighter. As the storm draws closer the wind starts to pick up and the sky darkens more and more. I can see the sand start to twirl into columns around us. Before we know it a loud crackle rings out from the left of us. As I turn to look I see one of the columns of sand get struck down by lightning. And, in a flash of light it's heated to a tall red hot glass spire. Loud rumbles and cracks ring out from all around us as more spires and lightning dot the sands around us. Suddenly, in front of us, lightning strikes a gust of sand and melts it into a spire. Maple yanks on the reins, trying to direct the Camsal out of the way, but as we draw closer I quickly grab the binoculars from Aeither's hands, and chuck them at the spire and it shatters. With its horn, the Camsal cracks through the remaining glass that's imbedded in the sand, as if it were nothing. Maple turns to me and gives a thumbs up, seemingly proud of my quick thinking. As we pass the rest of the storm nothing really

gets in our way. As the storm clears, the wind slows

down, and it is all a smooth ride from there on. We pass

dunes, more spires, and eventually we reach a port at a

canal. Maple guides his Camsal towards the stables, hops

off, and starts to talk to one of the workers at the stables. I

take the opportunity to dismount, Aeither follows me. I

stretch a bit, still feeling a bit stiff after holding onto the

saddle for so long. Maple seems to notice us hopping off.

"Ya'll can hop on a ferry! I'll be here if you need a ride

back!" he shouted. His tail sweeping the floor as he

seemed glad to help us get to Prius. I give him a wave

goodbye as I start to walk up the stairs. I look over and I

watch as Aeither shakes Maples hand and thanks him for

the ride before he catches up to me on the stairs. *"So, the*

lady I know, who might have some information for you,

lives in the south part of Prius; she goes by the name

Serpenti." he explains. I nod along. "*Serpenti.. Hmm alright. She sounds fancy.*" I added. Such a fancy name. I guess it's fitting since she lives in the city of pride. The newspaper house listings I saw in this place were insane. Massive houses with masterful architecture, bold colors, and lavish furniture.. All for the rich and elite. We reach the top of the stairs and hop aboard one of the ferries across the canal. It is strange, so many people dressed so fancy and just laughing and drinking. The city is one of endless festivals and parties it seems. I feel out of place in all of it, for one thing, my clothes are more casual than anything, and Aeither looked like a damn cowboy.. So, it seems neither of us fit in.. Eventually we reach the port once more. As I look out to the city I hear music, cheering, and laughing, just all the delights of parties. As the ferry docks we stumble our way through the crowd of other departing passengers. Aeither looks utterly ecstatic as he takes my hand and starts leading me down one of the streets through the city. It feels like Harenae, with the populated streets, the dancing people, the music and the vivid colors, except, turn the sound up by a million and add more drunk people.. We pass tons of bars, fancy clothing stores, and various other estabishments.

Despite all the joy around us, I feel some.. nervousness as we walk further into the city. Could this lead actually be the One? Could it be, after five years of my search, that there's finally justice for Azeroth? It's strange to think it. We continue up the street before Aeither turns to me and points to a house up on one of the hills. It's a massive mansion with marble walls and beautiful patterns engraved in the stone supports. *"That house up there is where she lives."* he explained. A soft smile on his face. *"That one? The real fancy one that looks like it belongs to a god?"* I muttered. Is he messing with me? It feels like he is, for the simple farm boy he appears to be, he knows quite a lot of people, more than I thought he would. He's a damn book of numbers and contacts it seems. He drags me further up the street until we stand at the door of this massive estate. I peek in through the windows and I see dozens of people, a massive party is occurring, how great.. But then I spot something, hundreds of fancily dressed Pavoleonem, the feathers on their tails sway as they walk down the stairs and I feel my heart drop. This is the house of a Royal Pride, a quite powerful one at that. I turn to Aeither before he can knock on the door. *"Aeither, you did not tell me that the 'Witness' was a part of a Royal Pride.."* I muttered. He chuckles a bit as he leans over a bit. *"Oh, come on, I said she lived in Prius. This place is fancy no matter what part.."* he mumbled. I glare down at him, how the hell is he acting so casual about this? *"Aeither, I look like I'm a bartender at a low end club and you look like you farm carrots! Do you really think they're gonna let us in with no complications or even an invitation?"* I hissed. He gives me a small 'calm down' kind of gesture with his hands. *"Hey, hey I know them well. They won't mind me stopping by.."* he mutters. He then knocks on the door and before I know it a butler appears. He looks us up and down before he turns to Aeither. *"Sir Aeither, what brings you to Prius?"* he questioned. I look over to Aeither just feeling… utterly confused. Does he know these people? Personally, at that? *"Hey Al, just looking for Serpenti, is she here?"* he questioned. That stupid pizzazz in his voice as he spoke.. The butler nods and opens the door further for us to step inside. *"Indeed, up at the third room to the left on the second floor."* he describes. We step inside and we pass crowds of partygoers, butlers with trays of drinks, and performers. It's quite a lavish gathering, one I could never imagine being in and yet here I am.. We walk up the steps and toward the third room to the left of the hallway. Aeither knocks on the door and a tall Pavoleonin woman steps out; she looks down at us, her expression more of a spiteful glare you'd get from a tip blocker at a bar before it softens into a smile as she notices Aeither. *"Ahh Aeither it's been quite some time hasn't it?"* she coos. She then turns to me with the same soft smile on her face. *"I see you have a guest as well. What may be your name dear?"* she asks as she reaches a paw out for a handshake. I took her hand and gave it a gentle shake. *"My name is Rune. I was told that you may have some valuable information on the murder of my lover, Azeroth."* I answered. She nods as her expression softens. She then steps out of the room and gestures for us to follow her down the hall. Next, she leads us to a stairwell, a heavily guarded one. Two bodyguards by the entrance to the stairwell glare us down but give us a pass to enter as Serpenti alerts them that we are her guests. We walk up the stairway which is lined top to bottom with bodyguards. As we walk, Serpenti turns to me. *"I must say I'm awfully sorry for what happened to your lover dear.. I've heard about your search; it's gone across the lands through words of many. 'A feathered one searching for the murderer of their dear lover'. It struck the hearts of us all.*

Azeroth was a close friend of my mother's you see, and after her death my mother suggested that we assist in your search. We would have contacted you sooner but.. we couldn't ever find you.." she murmured, her voice sounding remorseful. I.. never knew that she was close friends with this person's mother.. I knew she had friends from all across the lands, but she never really talked about them to me. She must've meant a lot to them. Maybe even close to as much as she did to me. We reach the top floor of the building and Serpenti motions the guards to open a large door. As they creep open, we are greeted with a large room. The walls are lined with gold adornments and paintings, the floor of the room was a shiny marble tile that clacked against my talons with each step I took inside. But to my main surprise, in the farther end of the room, lounging on a velvet chaise was a fancy lion of high status. The King of Pride himself.. It truly can't be! Really?

Is it truly him?

It feels unreal. **Prince**.. The literal god of pride is right in front of us. He rises from his chaise, the long feathers on his tail splay out like a fan as they flutter. *"Ah Serpenti my dear follower.. Is this the Rune that I've been told about?"* he announces. God his voice is booming. He could stand on a stage and wouldn't even need a microphone to get his growling voice across the room.. Serpenti nods. *"Yes, yes sir."* she replies. Prince steps forward and reaches his large finger out for some kind of handshake it seems. I take his finger and attempt to shake it at least. Aeither chuckles a bit at my struggle, and I glare at him with an annoyed look plastered on my face. Prince chuckles as he withdraws his hand and walks over to a table, gesturing to us to come over and sit down. We sit down and he opens a drawer and pulls out a folder with his claws, then slides it over to me. I opened it and its pictures.. Pictures from that night. I flip through all the pictures and my eyes stumble upon one in particular. It has what looks to be a cloaked figure, with bright white and gold wings with some strange patterns on it. It looked ethereal. But this was definitely who took the life of my lover. I can barely mutter a word, but it seems the lord of pride has some to share. *"These were taken by one of the managers in trade that I had stationed in Solmacula that night. They managed to capture these photos before the assailant fled. They said that they saw them disappear in a flash of light. That's why the officials in Solmacula couldn't find out where they went."* he explains as he taps one of the photos, which looks to be one of a blinding light. I'm just silent. That's why they couldn't find them, they disappeared. But how? *The blinding light doesn't tell me anything or..* *"But.. I do have an idea on how that light might tie into something."* he adds. He leans in a bit as he speaks in a hushed whisper. *"Now, **do not** tell any other mortal about this,* understand?" he commands, I nod along. "*Good. so, Azulon, the god of Guilt, manages the guilt of the people here, and the overworld too. And he sends very specific and highly trained personnel to go to the other side and gather intel on the mortals who reside in the overworld.. And they, with the right power or attuned object can traverse to and from the overworld and underworld with ease. And-* **do not tell him this but**- *I do believe that flash of light is from one of the stones he gives to his 'Observers'. These stones are crafted by his flame, and when they are used they emit a rather bright light, similar to the one the assailant had when they disappeared..*" he muttered. It.. all makes sense now. It's one of the 'Observers'. It has to be. "*The Observers.. Azulons Keep.. I have to go to Azulons Keep! I have to question him on this!*" I blurt out as I stand up. My wings flutter from just the sheer emotional whiplash I'm experiencing. After all this time, a genuine lead.. However, Prince stops me.

"Woah don't ruffle your feathers just yet. Azulon he's...

not.. The greatest to barge right in on.. You see, he's kind

of a... how do I put this.." he sighs as he moves to rub the

bridge of his muzzle. *"Whenever he even shows up for one*

of the meetings for all us gods he's.. Cynical..

Misanthropic and pessimistic.. Like a downer at a party

who's taking his annoyance for his messy breakup out on

*everyone else.. And especially if it's a **mortal** bothering*

him.. So, I'd recommend against it.. Maybe try and look for

an Observer themself? There's usually some who are off

their contracts for breaks in Harenae that you can talk to."

he explains. My brow furrows, the chances of one even

being on break at Harenae are low and that's a chance I'm

not willing to take. But for now, I nod as I take the two

pictures that catch my eye and slide them into my pocket. I

get up from my seat. *"Thank you for showing me this.*

Truly. I don't think there's any way I could ever repay

you.." I mutter. Prince nods as he holds out his finger for a

final handshake. "*Don't worry, justice for a close one*

comes free of charge here.." he replies. I shake his hand

or.. technically, finger as a last sign of respect. I then turn

away and gesture Aeither to come with and Serpenti

follows. Aeither notices the look on my face and he looks

a bit.. concerned, maybe. I couldn't care less. I have my

lead. And I'm doing everything in my power to follow it.

He catches up to me as we walk back down the stairs.

"*Alright! We're going back to Harenae to look for an*

Observer." he expressed. The same goofy smile on his

face that he gave me before. I think he's at least attempting

to cheer me up. "*No, we're going to Azulons Keep and*

have a word with that damn big lizard himself.." I hissed

out. Aeither seems a bit taken aback by my statement. "*Oh,*

come on, you heard the big cat man up there! Azulon's

kind of an asshole.. And I think it'd be safer for you **and** *me to not poke the big lizard with multiple arms for answers when he probably isn't going to give us one..*" he exclaimed. I give him a glare. "*You said that you would bring me here, not follow along with my troubles.*" I scold; I couldn't help but let the feathers on my wings puff up from the irritation I was feeling. Serpenti just seemed awkward from the little argument we were having.. "*Well, I wanna help you more. I'd like to stick with you cause it looks like you need some help with this.*" he added. I watch as his ears twitch every now and then as we continue to make our way down some more stairs and through the bustling party. I exit the house and Aeither stays behind a bit to say goodbye to Serpenti before catching up to me as I walk down the street. "*Hey, don't be like that alright? I'm trying to help you and I can't if you're gonna leave me behind like that..*" he mumbled, I sigh as I stop on the sidewalk and turn to him, rubbing the bridge of my nose as I speak. *"I do not **need** your help. You gave me the lead you said you would take me to, and that's it. If you want to stay and get dragged into my mess, then so be it.. But stay out of my way for the most part."* I hissed. The feathers along my back puff up once more as I keep getting more frustrated than I should. I turn my back on him once more and we continue to walk. We pass the once comforting streets, the same drunken people, the fancy dressed dancers and groups of friends laughing while sharing a drink. We then make it back to the pier and hop back on a ferry. The way back felt... more somber. The passengers aboard were quieter, softer. They recollected their night in the city with gratitude and they just hung close together. Me and Aeither however, stuck apart. I was annoyed. Rightfully so, in my eyes. I was taken to Prius, and that's all he promised. I don't know why he even wants to stay here along with me and my utter mess of getting justice. I've been searching for years for something: a clue, a lead, or anything, and I'm not taking the chance for any reason for another lead to just slip out of my hands like melting butter, due to some pissy lizard that I can easily get to give me answers. My heart grows old with the oil that she gave to fuel me, but I can only use it now to burn the things around me with my fiery wrath with a single spark from the thought of a lead, or getting justice for her death. And that oil in my heart is already heating at the thought of gathering more information on that damn Observer that fled like a coward. I ache for the day I'll be able to splay that damn coward across the stars like a gory arrow shot from the bow of Apollo himself. But my train of thought is interrupted as Aeither pats my shoulder as the other passengers scuffle off the ferry. I get up from my seat and we walk off. We make our way down the steps we once walked before, and I turn to my left to see Maple once more. He seems to be sending off his last delivery to someone as he turns over and notices us. He gives us a wave and gestures to us to come over. I walk over and he gives me a gentle smile. *"So, how'd it go for y'all?"* he questioned. I look down at him as I look off to the stables. *"Good. I got a lead. And we could use a ride back to Harenae. "*I muttered. He seems happy for me as he walks over to the stables to let out his Camsal. *"Nice! Whatcha plan on doin' back at Harenae, if I may ask? Got another person to visit?"* he queries. I'm unsure if I should tell him.. Because, first off, what we could be doing may be rather looked down upon or straight up illegal. *"I'll get into the details later.."* I mumble. He nods as he brings out his Camsal and mounts it, me and Aeither hop on and the trek back to Harenae begins.. As we pass through the small plains between the port and the Mare Harenae, everything is silent. Maple seems to notice the underlying tension, but he doesn't bother saying anything. He just continues the ride until we make it to the sand once more. He yanks the reins and the Camsal digs itself under the sand and begins to race through the ground again. I feel the familiar wind pelt against my face as we race through the sand. It's a lot cooler at night.. But it's eerie.. It's so quiet. Not the sounds of distant winds, storms or anything. Just the darkness, the dust trail from the Camsal swimming through the sand, and us. Maple turns to me a bit. *"So, I'm still curious. Why y'all headin' back to Harenae?"* he questions. However, he seems a bit hesitant to ask, probably due to the tension between me and Aeither. I sigh as I decide to give him the truth. *"We're going to Azulons Keep. The clues that we were given suggested that the murderer was one of his Observers. So, we're going to talk to that big lizard himself."* I explained. His expression seems to falter a bit as his eyes widen. *"Azulon? The big man himself? Really?!"* he blurts out, seemingly a bit taken aback by my statement. He then stutters a bit. *"Well, uh.. you see he ain't too kind with visitors.. Or uh.. Anyone really.."* he mumbles. It gets me thinking however. How does **he** know this? It's reasonable for another god like Prince to know that, but him? *"Well how do you know that, if I may ask?"* I ask, my tone feigning slight suspicion. He sighs a bit as his shoulders droop a bit. *"Well, uh, you know how all these gods n' such have accomplices? Like people who'll take over their job as god of whatever whenever they pass on or become another representative right? Well, uh I'm **technically** the accomplice of Azulon. But he kinda just.. sent me out to do my own thing cause he said I 'kept getting' in his way' of his work.."* he muttered quietly. It seems like it's a bit of a sensitive topic to him. *"W-wait, wait so you're telling me.. that if he passes on or*

*something.. **You'd** become the God of Guilt?"* I question..
My curiosity has now peaked. I don't know much about the
system of the gods; how they transfer their leadership or
their roles and such is all foreign to me. *"Well technically
yeah.."* he mumbles. I feel tempted to ask if he can take us
to Azulons Keep. He'd be the one to know it. *"Hey is it..
possible that you could take us there? To Azulons Keep?.."*
I mutter. I look at his face as I gauge his response, and it
doesn't seem like a good one. He's quiet for a moment as
his expression hardens to a look of deep thought. He then
sighs and his expression softens. *"Alright, I'll getcha'
there.. Uh, just don't mention me, alright? He'd be pissed
if I came back in there."* he muttered quietly. He grips the
reins and yanks them left, sending the Camsal to swim to
the left and off course of the city. He takes us past more
and more fulgar spires. Each growing larger and more
exotic the closer we got to.. Whatever is this place?.. As I

look up I see the flicker of thunder in a swirling cloud ahead. A large storm it seems. As we drew closer I spot more glass spires all around us; these however were much larger, much more complex. and they looked to be from much larger spirals of sand. Like a beautiful yet threatening display that echoes as an omen to what's to follow beyond the twisting clouds and sand. As we go further into the storm the wind picks up. I look to my left, and there are ten, maybe even twenty, large spirals of sand that collide into each other and dance around, some getting struck by lightning to form these massive multicolored spirals. *"Big man must be pissed if the storms are this bad.. Are you sure you wanna go there?"* he shouts, he's desperately trying to keep his voice from getting drowned out by the loud winds and thunder. I nod. *"Yes! It's the only way I think I'll get a legitimate answer."* I shouted. As I look ahead I see a massive mound of sand. It's covered from top to bottom with fulgar spires before they stop at an entrance to a cave. Maple carefully guides his Camsal into the cave. It gently digs itself out of the sand and begins to walk cautiously further down the cave. It's quiet. Eerily so. The cave's walls are lined with orange clay and old scripture that I can barely make out. It looks like it was drawn in with a single claw. Maybe Azulon himself or some other godly being. I recognize some of the symbols and drawings, it looks to be of the various gods emerging from a star. **Azulon, Valarie, Ragnar, Prince, and Bezzle,** emerging from a star labeled in an unknown string of letters. The next few drawings look to be of the past gods, the ones even before the five that we have now. I can't name any of them, they were way before my time and even my era. Some appear to be fighting, some overthrowing the other, or transferring their role it seems. All this history, just laid out in front of us in scripture that's been resting here untouched and unread, possibly for centuries. I look over to Aeither, who seems just as enamored by the drawings as I am. He points to one of the drawings. *"Isn't that one Azulon?"* he questioned. As I look up at it my eyes slide over the drawing. It looks like he's holding orbs in his hands, like massive pearls that he glares into. I believe it is. I look over to Maple. He seems nervous. The tension is palpable as we continue our descent. I look at the wall once more and read some of the drawings again. The one my eyes focus on is a series of gods who are receiving a gift of sorts from the star. Ragnar and Divina are given the gift of a daughter, Bezzle is given the gift of a son, Prince is given the gift of a daughter, Valarie is given the gift of knowledge, and Azulon is given the gift of a son. I glance at Maple. Maple.. He's the Forerunner of Guilt! The star patterns on his neck seem to connect to that realization. A gift from the stars. A gift that wasn't wanted. That's why he never wanted to come back here, why he didn't want us mentioning him. I feel.. bad for him. Maple pulls on the reins and the Camsal comes to a stop. Even the poor animal looks nervous. Maple looks back at us. He seems like he was thinking a lot as he gestures for us to get off. *"Alright.. Y'all here. Just.. be safe alright?"* he muttered quietly. Giving us a soft smile as we depart and walk further down the cave. We're soon greeted with a massive library of sorts with hundreds of behemoth shelves lined with hundreds of orbs, which are as large as my head and chest combined. It looks really, really, old, like an ancient tomb of knowledge, these orbs, and shelves. The ground shakes and I quickly pull Aether to the side behind one of the bookshelves. A loud vicious voice echoes out through the area. *"Damn these incoherent petty beings! Constantly squabbling and making my job increasingly more demanding than it already is.. I would go there myself and wipe them clean if it would clear me of this horrid job and role..*" it mutters out. The ground shakes more as large steps come our way. As I look up, I'm greeted by the horrific sight of Azulon himself. He grumbles as he picks up one of the orbs on the highest of the shelves and breathes a puff of blue flame onto it. The orbs color smoothens into a deep purple. Quite a contrast from the deep red it was before. He sets it down before crawling off to another shelf. The footsteps get quieter as he steps away, and I turn to Aeither. *"We need to get somewhere higher, so we don't get trampled.."* I mutter to him as I turn my attention to one of the ladders leading to a higher level on the parallel shelves. *"That one. Go use that ladder."* he murmured. He walks over to the edge of the shelf and peeks out. Looking around a bit before he suddenly dashes out towards the ladder. I rush after him, nearly tripping over one of the floorboards as we run for the ladder. We climb up it. But as I draw halfway up, I begin to feel nervous. I desperately try not to look down as I shakily make my way up. I barely get to the top and I climb to sit on the shelf. I take a few breaths as I look over to Aeither who's peeking out from behind one of the orbs. *"We.. we gotta get his attention.."* I say breathlessly. I get up and I try to wave him down. Azulon makes his way through the library of orbs, but he doesn't even notice us. He walks away from the shelves we stand on, opting instead, to go to the other side of the library.. How great.. Not only is he a jerk; he can barely notice anything strange. *"He didn't see us.. Great.."* I mumble angrily as my arms drop down to my sides. I look over to Aeither and his expression lightens up. He grins as he seems to have an idea. He then starts to push the orb he was hiding behind. *"Wait, what are you doing?"* I hissed. But before I can stop him the orb plops off its stand, rolls off the shelf, and falls to the floor, shattering. A loud crackle rings out through the library, and I close my eyes momentarily. Did he just do that?.. Before I can even scold him, loud footsteps echo closer, and the floor starts to shake. I peer out to the end of the hall, and I can see Azulon stomping his way over. Oh boy.! As he sees the shattered orb on the ground, he roars angrily. He walks over to the shattered remnants of the orb and begins to pick up the larger chunks with one of his four hands. Aeither then calls out to him from the top shelf. *"Hey, uh sorry about that but we need your help!"* he shouts out. I look at him in utter disbelief. How stupid is he?.. First, he breaks something, then he's yelling an apology at a literal god?? Oh lord.. *"Aeither I swear to Valerie himself, what in actual hell are you doing? Are you trying to get us killed?!"* I scolded him. His expression, which was once proud drops, to more of a guilty, worried one. And that expression really fits what's happening because, to my right, Azulon raises his head. He glares at both of us rather angrily.

"What in your mind gave you the right to enter my keep?!"

he roars as one of his hands swipes the ladder out of the

way, taking the option of leaving off the table now. I turn

to face this utter behemoth of a god, and I take a breath. I

pull out the photos from my pocket and hold them out. *"I*

am Rune. my lover was murdered in the night by what I

believe is one of your Observers." I shout, waving the two

pictures in the air. He leans to the side a bit. His large eye

observes the photo as his brow furrows and his muzzle lifts

to an annoyed snarl. He tilts his head down to rub the

bridge of his nose in annoyance. *"So, you broke in here,*

trespassed on the God of Guilt's property, over a photo of

a bright light and some cloaked figure, because you think

they have something from me? God, I cannot believe

mortals and their stupid, stupid intuitions.." he growls.

"Sir, the crystals, the stones that you give to your

Observers glow when they are used. They glow just like the light the murderer of my lover used. One of your observers killed my lover and I demand justice for her death!" I shout back in retaliation; I feel my wings unconsciously splay out from just how pissed off I am. How can he be so ignorant? He rolls his eyes as he glances towards the photos again. *"You are aware that the light my stones emit were **never** that bright, correct? They're simply a small increase of light, not this whole rapturing thing that your little murderer did.. And yet you storm in here and, with the least respect, accuse one of my Observers which- I don't even know how you know of them in the first place- of murdering another mortal which is the least of my concerns as a god."* he exclaims angrily. He then turns his unwavering glare towards Aeither. *"And then, you have the audacity to drag others into your little sob story.."* he adds. Aeithers expression shows offense as he interrupted him. *"Hey, I'm here willingly! They had something wrongfully* *taken from them, all us mortals have. And you're just gonna what, run around this library of damn crystal balls as you complain about your job as a god, when you never witness the struggle of the mortals above because you're too busy huddled in your keep?"* he shouted in retaliation. Azulon chuckles a bit. His lips pulled back to a snarl as he spoke. *"So, then you won't mind this.."* he scoffs as his hands suddenly reach out and grab us. He begins to walk toward the balcony of this floor, he doesn't even express worry or botherance at us trying to get out of his grasp. I begin to panic as we draw closer to the edge of the railing. He holds us over the edge. As I look down I see a massive pool of water. However, something is off about it. It swirls in a whirlpool and, the closer the water draws to the funnel, it deepens into a dark purple. The sound of whooshing water is all I hear before Azulon begins to speak. *"The people of Harenae. Notice how they're as content as possible, living their lives despite being in the heart of guilt? Their own hearts ache, but they live, they continue, they love even with hearts of iron and rust that have been oxidized over and over again by the drips of ache. So, tell me, 'great' feathered Rune, why hasn't your heart stopped for a moment to stop rusting? It seems for years you've been simmering in your own self regret for not being able to save your lover, but that never gave you the right to drag the people around you down into your spiral of insanity. You followed the string to truth, but I swear, by all my godly might, that it will lead you to nothing but the death of yourself and others! So, take this as a gift, a gift for you to reflect on, and stop before you get yourself too deep in trouble.."* he preaches. His gaze unwavering as he releases his grip, and we fall from his grasp. My hands reach out in a spark of hope that I'll be pulled back. But as I splash into the water, I know that there isn't a chance of me being saved. I'm not meant to be.. I try to swim to the surface, but I'm dragged down by the whirlpool. And before I can comprehend what's happening, or call out to Aeither, I'm dragged down deeper. And everything goes dark around me.

To be continued..

Still to come:

Shifting Tides

Queen of Wrath

Remembrance

The Deities Lament

Made in the USA
Middletown, DE
26 July 2024

57791184R00050